# A NOTE TO PARENTS

When your children are ready to "step into reading," giving them the right books is as crucial as giving them the right food to eat. **Step into Reading Books** present exciting stories and information reinforced with lively, colorful illustrations that make learning to read fun, satisfying, and worthwhile. They are priced so that acquiring an entire library of them is affordable. And they are beginning readers with a difference—they're written on five levels.

**Early Step into Reading Books** are designed for brand-new readers, with large type and only one or two lines of very simple text per page. **Step 1 Books** feature the same easy-to-read type as the Early Step into Reading Books, but with more words per page. **Step 2 Books** are both longer and slightly more difficult, while **Step 3 Books** introduce readers to paragraphs and fully developed plot lines. **Step 4 Books** offer exciting nonfiction for the increasingly independent reader.

The grade levels assigned to the five steps—preschool through kindergarten for the Early Books, preschool through grade 1 for Step 1, grades 1 through 3 for Step 2, grades 2 through 3 for Step 3, and grades 2 through 4 for Step 4—are intended only as guides. Some children move through all five steps very rapidly; others climb the steps over a period of several years. Either way, these books will help your child "step into reading" in style!

*For Lillian, with love*
— *M. K.*

*For Katie and Jennie Rose*
— *D. P.*

Text copyright © 1997 by Monica Kulling
Illustrations copyright © 1997 by Diane Paterson
Published in the United States by Random House, Inc., New York, and simultaneously
in Canada by Random House of Canada Limited, Toronto.

http://www.randomhouse.com/

*Library of Congress Cataloging-in-Publication Data*
Kulling, Monica. Marmee's surprise : a Little women story / based on the novel by
Louisa May Alcott ; adapted by Monica Kulling. p. cm. — (Step into reading. A step 3 book)
SUMMARY: Even though their father is away at war and the family does not have much money,
the four March sisters manage to have a wonderful Christmas. ISBN 0-679-87579-4 (pbk.) —
ISBN 0-679-97579-9 (lib. bdg.) [1. Sisters—Fiction. 2. Christmas—Fiction.] I. Alcott, Louisa May,
1832–1888. Little women. II. Title. III. Series: Step into reading. Step 3 book. PZ7.K9490155Mar
1997 [Fic]—dc20  95-30266

Printed in the United States of America  10 9 8 7 6 5 4 3 2 1

STEP INTO READING is a registered trademark of Random House, Inc.

Step into Reading®

# Marmee's Surprise

## A LITTLE WOMEN STORY

Based on the novel by
Louisa May Alcott

Adapted by Monica Kulling
Illustrated by Diane Paterson

A Step 3 Book

Random House 🏠 New York

## Chapter One

Usually, the March family loved Christmas. Every year, Father would bring home a great big tree. Marmee would sing carols and hang up the stockings. The four sisters would bake gingerbread cookies and decorate the tree.

Meg was the oldest March sister. She liked to make long garlands of popcorn. Tomboy Jo would put up the lights. Beth hung ornaments on each branch. And little Amy always topped the tree with a special star.

But this year was different. Father was far away, fighting in a war. He would not be home for the holidays. And the family was too poor to buy presents.

The March sisters tried to make the best of things. They did not have a tree. But they could still bake gingerbread cookies.

"It's awful to be poor," said Meg. She remembered when the family had more money.

"It won't feel like Christmas without presents," grumbled Jo.

"Some girls have lots of pretty things," said little Amy. "But other girls have nothing at all!"

Beth chimed in, "We've got Father and Mother and each other."

But the sisters knew that Beth was only half-right. They *were* lucky to have such a wonderful family. But they might not see Father for a long time. He and the other soldiers were probably very sad and lonely.

"The holidays won't be the same
without Father," agreed Meg. "And
without presents. There are so many
pretty things I want."

"*I* know," said Jo. "We each have a
dollar. We could buy something for
ourselves."

Jo was a bookworm. She already knew
which book she would buy.

"Let's do it!" said Meg.

"I'm going to buy new piano music,"
announced Beth.

"I want a new box of drawing pencils,"
said Amy. "I really need them!"

Suddenly the girls were excited. They
would have Christmas presents after all!

## Chapter Two

The grandfather clock in the hall struck six. Mother would soon be home! Beth found her slippers. Meg lit the lamp. Amy jumped up from Marmee's favorite easy chair. Jo moved over to the hearth. She held the slippers close to the warm fire.

"These slippers are worn out," said Jo. "Marmee needs a new pair."

"I'll buy Marmee a new pair of slippers!" said Beth. "I don't need new music."

"No, I will!" cried Amy.

Meg added, "But I'm the oldest—"

"Papa told *me* to take care of Marmee," Jo cut in. "*I* will buy the slippers."

Beth stopped the fight. She had the best idea.

"Let's not get anything for ourselves," she said. "Let's *each* buy Marmee something instead!"

The girls forgot about their wish lists. There was one thing they wanted more. They wanted their loving Marmee to be happy on Christmas Day.

"We'll go shopping tomorrow," said Jo. "Marmee will think we are buying presents for ourselves. She will be *so* surprised!"

Each girl thought of a special gift. A pair of slippers! A pair of gloves! White handkerchiefs! A bottle of perfume! They giggled with delight over the plans.

"I'm glad my girls are so merry," said a cheery voice at the door. It was Marmee. She had been at the Soldiers' Aid Society. She went there every day to pack first-aid boxes for the soldiers.

Marmee took off her bonnet and cloak.

"I've got a wonderful surprise," she said. "A letter from Father! I'll read it to you after dinner."

Jo jumped to her feet. "A letter! A letter! Three cheers for Father!"

The March sisters wanted to hear Father's letter. They hurried to get dinner ready. Amy bustled around the house and told everyone what to do. Meg arranged the tea. Beth buttered the biscuits. Jo set the table.

The girls ate quickly. They hardly
tasted the food. Beth finished first and
waited patiently for the others. Amy and
Meg chattered about what Father might be
eating for *his* dinner. Jo was so excited that
she dropped her bread on the floor.

After dinner, the girls gathered by the fire. Mother read Father's letter aloud. It was full of hope and good wishes.

Father missed the whole family. He thought about them every day. He told the girls about life in the army. He told them about the men and the long marches.

Marmee folded the letter. She tucked it into her pocket. Her eyes were misty with tears. Everyone was quiet, thinking about Father. They missed him too! If only he could be home for Christmas.

"Living without Father is hard," said Marmee. "You need to be strong."

"I want to try very hard to be a little woman," said Jo. "I wish we had something to show us how."

"Look under your pillows on Christmas morning," said Marmee as she left the room. Her eyes twinkled. But she said no more.

After Marmee went upstairs, it was time for chores. The girls pulled out their work baskets and started to sew sheets for their Aunt March. Usually, the girls complained about the dull work. But tonight, they pretended the sheets were continents. They talked about all the magnificent countries they were stitching through.

After all the chores were done, Marmee joined the girls at the piano. Beth hopped up on the bench and began to play. Everyone sang their favorite songs.

Marmee and Meg had lovely voices.

Their singing sounded like flutes. Amy chirped like a cricket. Jo liked to sing, too. Her voice sometimes cracked and went off-key. But none of the Marches minded. They loved every member of their little choir.

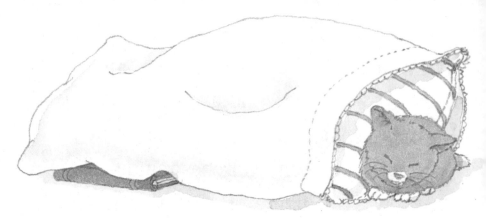

## Chapter Three

Christmas morning was bright and snowy.
Jo was the first one awake. She looked
under her pillow for Marmee's surprise.
It was a red Bible.

Soon all the sisters woke up. Each girl
found a Bible under her pillow. The books
were decorated with Christmas colors.
Marmee had written a special message
inside each one. The March sisters loved
their gifts!

"Let's read a little every morning," said
Meg. "It would be a wonderful way to start
the day."

The other girls agreed. They eagerly
opened their books and read.

An hour later, the girls went down to the kitchen. Marmee's Christmas breakfast was already on the table.

"Merry Christmas!" said Marmee.

Then she added, "Girls, I am worried about Mrs. Hummel."

Marmee told them the sad story of their neighbor, poor Mrs. Hummel. Mrs. Hummel had six children and a newborn baby. She did not have enough food to feed them all. Marmee wanted to help the Hummel family.

"My girls, will you give them your breakfast as a Christmas present?" asked Marmee.

The girls were very hungry. Christmas breakfast was their favorite meal. But it did not take them long to decide.

"We'll help carry the things to the poor children," said Beth, eagerly.

"I will take the cream and the muffins," added Amy.

Meg wrapped up the bread and the buckwheat pancakes.

The March girls and Marmee hurried
over to the Hummels.

"Mama, are they angels?" asked the
grateful Hummel children.

The four March sisters had never been called angels before. They gave Mrs. Hummel the food and giggled all the way home.

"That's loving our neighbor," said Meg when they returned.

The girls had bread and milk for breakfast. But they were happy. They had done a good deed.

After breakfast, the girls gave Marmee her presents. Each present had a note tied to it. Marmee loved every single gift.

Marmee put the slippers on right away. She sprinkled perfume on the new handkerchief. She tucked the handkerchief into her pocket. She tried the gloves on. They fit perfectly!

"You are my wonderful, wonderful girls!" said Marmee joyfully.

There were no more presents for the girls. But it didn't matter. Marmee's smiling face was all they wanted.

# Chapter Four

Every Christmas, Jo wrote a play. This year, it was called *The Witch's Curse*. Each sister had a part. The girls built a stage. They made a forest out of plants and green cloth. They built a tower out of boxes.

That night, a dozen friends came to the March house to watch the play.

It was time! Beth and Amy pulled the curtain up.

Jo played Roderigo. Meg played Zara. Roderigo had to rescue the beautiful Zara from the evil Hugo.

Meg was trapped in a tall tower. Jo bravely climbed to the top. But the boxes were not sturdy enough. They wobbled under Jo's feet. The tower fell down. Jo and Meg landed on the floor under boxes!

The audience roared with laughter. But Jo just pushed the boxes aside. She stood up and said her next line. Her sisters followed her lead. The play went on. At the end, everyone clapped with glee.

After the play, there was another
Christmas surprise. It was a splendid feast!
The dining room table was covered
with food. There were bowls of pink and

white ice cream. There was cake and fruit and French candy. There were also four bunches of flowers—one for each March girl!

The feast took everyone's breath away.

"Did fairies bring this?" asked Amy.

"No, it was Santa Claus!" said Beth.

"I think Mother did it," said Meg.

But Mrs. March shook her head.

"Maybe Aunt March sent the feast over?" said Jo.

No one could guess. It wasn't fairies or
Santa Claus or Aunt March. The feast was
sent by Mr. Laurence. He was the Marches'
rich next-door neighbor. Mr. Laurence
lived with his grandson. They usually kept
to themselves. They never did anything for
their neighbors. Except tonight!

"I want to meet that Laurence boy," said Jo. "Maybe next year he will come to our play!"

"The new year may bring you a new friend," replied Marmee.

The March family and their guests sat
down to enjoy the delicious dinner. They
touched glasses and made a toast to happy
days ahead.

One by one, the sleepy little women crawled into bed. Christmas had been full of wonderful surprises. The March family did not have much money. But they were very lucky. They were rich in friends and laughter and love.